This book belongs to

_____

First published in Great Britain by HarperCollins Publishers Ltd in 1995. ISBN 0 00 198184 6 (hardback) 10 9 8 7 6 5 4 3 2 1
ISBN 0 00 664583 6 (paperback) 10 9 8 7 6 5 4 3 2 1   Text and illustrations copyright © Mark Burgess 1995

Teddy and Rabbit's
Picnic Outing

Mark Burgess

Collins

An Imprint of HarperCollinsPublishers

Teddy and Rabbit were getting ready for Crocodile's picnic when Penguin came into the shop. He was looking rather fed up.
"What's the matter, Penguin?" asked Rabbit.
"I don't know," said Penguin.

"Cheer up!" said Teddy. "We're all invited to Crocodile's picnic and look what a lovely sunny day it is."

"I don't care about picnics or sunny days," said Penguin.

"I'll do a little dance for you,"
said Rabbit. "Perhaps that will
cheer you up."
"It might," said Penguin.

Rabbit danced for Penguin.
"I'm a bit out of practice," she said,
but Penguin didn't look quite so
unhappy.

Mouse came into the shop.
"Why Penguin, you look sad," said
Mouse. "What's the matter?"
"He doesn't know," said Rabbit.
"That's right," said Penguin.
"I don't know."

"Magic tricks are good for cheering people up," said Mouse. "Let me show you one."

Mouse's trick went a bit wrong
but Penguin smiled all the same,
just a tiny bit.

Elephant came into the shop.
"Hello," said Elephant.
"Penguin is feeling sad," said Mouse.
"We're trying to cheer him up."
"Jokes are good for cheering people
up," said Elephant. "Let me tell
you one."

Elephant
began
to tell
his joke...

but he couldn't
remember how
it went.

"Oh dear," said Elephant. "I'm sorry."
But Penguin laughed all the same,
rather a lot.

Crocodile came into the shop.
"So here you all are," she said. "I've
been looking for you everywhere."

"Penguin was feeling sad," said Elephant. "We've been cheering him up."

"That's right," said Penguin, "but I'm all right now."

"Good," said Crocodile. "Then let's go for our picnic."

"Yes, let's!" said Penguin.